D0499913

Lilly's Good Deed

Brenda Bellingham

Lilly's Good Deed

Illustrations by Kathy Kaulbach

The New Series

Formac Publishing Limited
Halifax, Nova Scotia

The development and pre-publication work on this project was
funded in part by the Canada/Nova Scotia Cooperation
Agreement on Cultural Development.

First publication in the United States, 1999

Formac Publishing Company Limited acknowledges the support
of the Canada Council and the Nova Scotia Department of
Education and Culture in the development of writing and
publishing in Canada.

Canadian Cataloguing in Publication Data

Bellingham, Brenda, 1931-

   Lilly's good deed

   (First novels. The new series)

ISBN 0-88780-460-8 (pbk.) —ISBN 0-88780-461-6
(bound)

I. Kaulbach, Kathy R. (Kathy Rose), 1955- II. Title. III.
Series.

PS8553.E468L55   1998   jC813;.54   C98-950217-1

PZ7.B4142Li 1998

Formac Publishing
Limited
5502 Atlantic Street
Halifax, NS B3H 1G4

Distributed in the U.S. by
Orca Book Publishers
P.O. Box 468 Custer, WA
U.S.A. 98240-0468

Printed and bound in Canada

Table of Contents

1
Theresa Green

At recess, Kendall and Heathrow kept running through our skipping rope. We girls yelled at them, but we didn't really mind. They were only trying to tease.

It was Minna's turn to skip when Theresa Green raced in from nowhere. She wasn't even supposed to be playing. She crashed into Minna, who is small and pretty and my best friend. Minna went flying. She hurt her ankle and couldn't stand up.

Heathrow ran to help her. He's new to our school. He was born at Heathrow airport when his family was travelling from India, so his family nicknamed him Heathrow. My mother says he's a real gentleman. I think he's cool.

Kendall went to help Heathrow. Kendall isn't a real gentleman, but he tries to copy Heathrow. Between them they grabbed wrists and made a seat for Minna and carried her into school. The rest of us bawled Theresa out.

"I didn't mean to knock her down," she whined. "It was an accident. I was only trying to bug you."

"You always bug us," I said. "You don't have to try." Theresa is always pushing people and she always says it's an accident. She calls me Bossy Boots, even

though I'm not anymore. She makes me mad.

After school Minna went home to practise her piano. I went home to peel potatoes and carrots for supper. My parents weren't home from work yet, so I went outside.

Minna couldn't come out because her ankle still hurt.

The Goodalls' cat, Muff, from next door, came to see me. She was white with blue eyes and very shy. I was the only kid she allowed to pet her. Cats are good judges of people, Mrs. Goodall said. I bet Muff wouldn't go anywhere near Theresa Green.

2
Dumb Name

I made up a new skipping rhyme. "Trees Are Green is so mean. Go away and don't be seen."

Pop — he's my stepfather — came home and heard me. "I don't like the sound of that rhyme," he said.

"I know," I said. "But it isn't easy to find something to rhyme with Green."

"I don't mean that," Pop said. "Her name is Theresa Green, not Trees Are Green. Some parents accidentally give their kids dumb names. It's not her fault."

"Right," I said.

Before my dad died, my name was Lilly Gilbert. No problem. Then Mom married Peter Otis Pond. They changed my name so I'd match the rest of the family.

"Lilly Pond!" I said. "THAT's a dumb name."

"I think it's pretty," Pop said. "Like you." He put his arm around my shoulder "What's eating you, Tiger? Why don't you like Theresa Green?"

I told him about her and Minna.

"Maybe you should ask her to play and then she wouldn't butt in," Pop said. "If you got to know her better, you might like her."

"I doubt it," I said.

Pop kissed the top of my head. "Let's start supper. Mom will be along soon."

We went in together. I couldn't help wondering if anyone ever hugged Trees Are Green. Or told her she was pretty, even though she wasn't. Or kissed her when she was being grouchy. I bet they didn't.

3
New Neighbors

"Hey, look," Kendall said, "there's a pick-up truck. The house across the street must have been rented."

"It has," Minna said. "The woman who's coming to live there works evenings. Grandma is going to babysit for her." We were on our way home from school, so we watched. A guy took a brand new two-wheeler out of his pick-up and wheeled it into the garage. He came out, locked the garage door and drove away.

"He looks like a real grouch," said Kendall.

"Maybe he isn't the new neighbour," Heathrow said, sounding hopeful. "He's just delivering the bike."

"I think he looks sad, not mad," I said.

"Why can't the kid who gets the bike babysit?" Kendall asked.

Minna looked puzzled. "I don't know. Grandma sometimes doesn't understand people very well on the phone."

At that moment a woman drove up and parked in front of the vacant house. She unloaded some boxes from the trunk and piled them on the sidewalk. Next she yanked open the passenger seat door. "I could use some help, Theresa," she said. "Hop to it."

Minna, Kendall, Heathrow and I froze. We watched to see who got out. You guessed it. Trees Are Green!

"Let's go, Heathrow," Kendall said. "I'm hungry."

"See you," Heathrow said to us. "Good luck, Minna."

"Theresa Green!" Minna groaned. "What am I going to do?"

"Tell your grandma what she's like," I said. "I bet she'd ask Mrs. Green to find another sitter."

"No," Minna said. "I don't want Grandma to know. She worries about me enough. Besides, she needs the money." She sighed. "I'll have to play with Theresa. How will I ever get time to practise?"

Minna's piano playing is awesome. She's going to be a concert pianist when she grows up. I know how much her piano means to her.

"I'll come over and help you play with her," I said.

4
Tiger Lilly

Next day, after school, I went home with Minna. Theresa Green's mother dragged her over to Minna's house. She didn't want to be there, and we didn't want to have her. I had to feel sorry for her.

That's when I remembered what Pop had said — that we should try to get to know her. Anyway, we couldn't just sit there not looking at one another.

"Let's play Barbie dolls," I said. "I've brought mine. You can share with me, Theresa."

"Your dolls are garbage, Bossy Boots," she said. "I'll play with Minnie Mouse's Barbies."

Minna's grandma had made their clothes. They looked like princesses.

Theresa tugged at a gorgeous emerald green, velvet gown. "Oops," she said. "I ripped something." Pretty soon there were tiny buttons and beads flying everywhere.

Minna looked at the mess. She was mad, but she was almost crying. I knew she was thinking of her grandma's work getting wrecked.

"I'm not playing anymore," she said, tossing back her hair. "I have to practise."

23

"Here, Minnie Mouse. Take your dumb Barbie," Theresa said, and she threw it down.

Minnie Mouse! Bossy Boots! Grrr. I might get to *know* Theresa, but I'd never get to *like* her. She made me feel like a tiger — the man-eating kind. Mom and Pop don't approve of fighting. There are better ways to solve a problem, they say. I had to get Theresa out of there before I forgot.

"Come on," I said. "We can ride bikes with Kendall and Heathrow." I could see them through the window.

"Okay, Bossy Boots," Theresa said.

5
Look Out, Muff!

Theresa dragged an old bike out of her garage. It was in even worse shape than mine.

"Why don't you ride your new bike?" I asked.

"Never in a million years," she cried. "HE gave it to me."

I remembered the guy we'd seen delivering the new bike. We hadn't seen him since. An idea struck me. "Who? Your dad?"

"None of your business, Bossy Boots," Theresa answered. "Anyway, he's not my my dad anymore. I hate him."

I didn't ask why. She wouldn't tell me, anyway. I got my bike and followed her into the street.

The top of our street is closed off, so there weren't many cars to bother us. Outside Theresa's house, the driveway had sunk. If you hit it fast enough, it made a great jump. You had to go up on the sidewalk first, but we always made sure it was empty.

"Wear your helmet," I told Theresa.

"I don't need to," she said.

"No helmet, no tricks," I said. Oops! I thought I'd stopped being a bossy boots.

"Okay, okay, Bossy Boots. I'll wear it," Theresa said.

Heathrow showed her what to do. Kendall just showed off.

"You can go next, if you like, Theresa," I said, trying to make up for being a bossy boots. She didn't smile, or say thank you or anything.

While I waited my turn, I watched Muff. She was across the road, chasing dead leaves in Mrs. Goodall's front yard. Cute little cat!

Finally, Trees Are Green gave me a turn. I pedalled faster and faster down the street, then up one of the driveways onto the sidewalk. Just then, Muff raced across the road. She was heading for Theresa's driveway, right across my path.

"Muff!" I screamed. "Look out."

6
An Accident

Muff was a very independent cat, Mrs. Goodall said. Actually, she was deaf. At the last moment, she saw me coming. She froze. I swerved. I missed Muff. Something bigger got in my way. Theresa Green! I swerved again. My front wheel hit the bump, sort of sideways. I fell off my bicycle and flew through the air.

If only Mrs. Mott hadn't come down her path just then!

Mrs. Mott lived next door to Theresa Green. She was elderly and didn't drive, so she was going to take the bus from the end of the street. She saw me coming and threw her arms around the tree at the edge of her lawn. I threw my arms around Mrs. Mott. I needed something to hang on to.

"Just you wait until I tell Adolphus about this," she screamed. "He'll have plenty to say to your parents."

That's when I knew I was in trouble. Usually she called her son Dolly.

"I'm really sorry," I said. "Someone ran in front of me." I glared at Theresa Green.

"You almost knocked me down," Mrs. Mott complained.

Heathrow, Kendall and I apologized like mad. Theresa

30

was too busy cuddling Muff. Muff didn't seem to mind a bit.

"I thought cats were supposed to know what people are like," I grumbled. Muff's disloyalty hurt, almost as much as my knees and elbows. Next day Adolphus came around, and our parents took away our bicycles for a week.

"It'll be snowing by then," Kendall said.

Every day, after school, Theresa raced us home. Minna and I were glad. At least we had some time together. "Grandma says it's hard for three to get along," Minna said. "She thinks it's better if Theresa does her homework and watches TV while I practise. I'm sorry, Lilly."

You'd have to be an angel to like Trees Are Green.

7
Lost Kitten

One day we caught up with Theresa Green at Mrs. Goodall's house.

"Have any of you girls seen a kitten?" Mrs. Goodall asked. "This morning I saw someone drop one on my front lawn. But by the time I'd dressed and got outside, it was gone. I've looked for it everywhere."

"That's so cruel," I cried. "I hate people who do that."

"I'd punch them out if I caught them," Theresa said.

Trees Are Green and I felt the same way about cats!

"Maybe she's not so bad after all," I said to Minna.

"She likes my music," Minna said. "I was going to tell you, but it seemed like boasting."

The next day was Friday. Heathrow, Kendall and I were on our way home from soccer practice when Theresa Green crawled out from under Adolphus Mott's car. Her face was black. Muff sat on top of the car watching.

"What's she doing?" I asked Heathrow and Kendall.

"Who cares?" Kendall said. "I'm hungry. Let's go."

"If she doesn't stop fooling about with that car, she'll be in big trouble," Heathrow said.

"Well, I'm not telling her to stop," I said. "She'll call me Bossy Boots."

"Mrs. Mott will send for the police," Heathrow said, "and Theresa will go to jail."

I could let her go to jail, or I could stop her. What should I do? I imagined her locked up in a little cell with only cold, greasy food to eat. "Come on," I said.

Heathrow and I ran across the road. Kendall walked.

"Listen, Trees are Green," I said, "you shouldn't touch that car. It isn't yours."

"It isn't yours either, Bossy Boots," she answered.

I wished I'd let her go to jail.

8
Lilly Writes a Note

"What are you doing?" Heathrow asked.

"There's a kitten under the hood," Theresa answered. "I'm trying to get it out."

"It must be the one Mrs. Goodall saw," I said. "Ask Dolly Mott to open the hood."

Theresa Green gave me a scornful look. "I tried that. Dolly and his mother have gone to a wedding. Mrs. Goodall saw them drive away in a taxi."

"Let me try," Heathrow said. He wriggled under the car and squirmed about. When he came

out his hand was bleeding. "I couldn't reach it," he said, "but I heard it mew."

Kendall called, "Kitty, kitty. Here, kitty."

I went to borrow some cat food from Mrs. Goodall. While I was there, she asked me to take Muff home.

"Dolly Mott hates to see paw marks on his car," she said. "He spends half his life polishing it."

The cat food didn't work either. It was getting dark, so Kendall and Heathrow had to go. Minna came to get Theresa. Mom called me home.

"What if Dolly comes home and starts his car?" Theresa said. "The kitten will get hurt. I'm not leaving."

I felt the same way, but I knew my parents wouldn't let me stay out all night.

Everybody looked at everybody else.

"I know!" I yelled. "We'll write a note and stick it to the car where Dolly can't miss it."

Heathrow had a pen in his pocket. Minna went for paper and sticky tape.

"DANGER!" I printed. "DO NOT START THIS CAR. KITTEN UNDER HOOD."

"Dolly doesn't care about cats," Theresa said. "He said you should have run over Muff, instead of running into his mother. He's a doughhead."

I crumpled up the first notice and tried again. "DANGER

BEFORE YOU START THIS CAR PHONE:"

"Put my phone number," said Theresa. "My house is right next door."

9
Don't Open This Car

We stuck one notice on the windshield and one on the window of the driver's door. That way Dolly couldn't miss them. Minna went home for more tape. We had to make sure the notes wouldn't blow off.

Next morning I jumped out of bed and ran to the window. Across the street stood Mrs. Mott and Dolly. Dolly was waving one of my notices. I could see his lips moving. Then he steered his mother up the path and into the house. Theresa's phone would be ringing any minute now.

I dragged on my jeans and T-shirt and phoned Minna. We didn't want to miss the rescue. We arrived at the same time as Theresa and Dolly. Mrs. Mott stayed inside.

Dolly had a fierce, black moustache and bushy eyebrows. One of my notices was still dangling from his thick, red fingers. "Who wrote this?" He smacked my note — printed on pink paper — with the back of his other hand.

"I did," I squeaked. He looked pretty scary.

"Crazy kid," he shouted. "You had me thinking there was a bomb under my car. Now I hear it's just a rotten cat."

"A little kitten," I said.

"That's no excuse to gum up my windows with miles of sticky tape and stupid notes."

Minna tossed her long black hair over her shoulder. "Please don't shout," she said. "Lilly had to save the kitten. We'll clean the sticky stuff off your windows."

Dolly glared at her and stuck his key in the lock. Theresa gave a shriek that sent a shiver down my spine. She rushed at Dolly. "Don't you dare start that car," she yelled. "You'll hurt the kitten."

Dolly staggered back against the car. His face got even redder. His collar suddenly looked too tight.

"Wait, Trees," I cried. "He's only going to open the hood. He doesn't want blood and guts and bits of fur all over his engine. After a while, it'll smell."

Minna looked sick. Theresa looked as if she was going to pound me instead of Dolly.

Dolly turned green. "Cool it, kid," he said to Theresa. "Like your friend said, I was just going to spring the hood."

10
Trees and Boots

Theresa and I sat on her front step. Minna had gone to her piano lesson. Theresa held the kitten. Her mother had said she could keep it. I wished I could have it, but I couldn't. Macdonald, my little brother, is allergic to cats. Muff purred against my leg. I picked her up.

"Why did you have to say all that gross stuff to Dolly Mott?" Theresa asked. "It'll give me nightmares."

"It was the only way to stop him," I said. "Dolly's really fussy about how his car looks."

Theresa grinned. "I bet he hates it when his mom calls him Dolly."

"Maybe not," I said. "Pop calls me Tiger and I call him Pop. That's because we like one another."

Theresa's grin turned to a scowl. "I hate my dad," she said.

"Pop's not my dad. He's my stepfather," I said. "I used to hate my dad, too, after he died. I was mad at him for leaving us, but he couldn't help it."

"My dad could help it," Theresa said. "He went to work in a foreign country."

"I bet he didn't want to," I said. "I saw him, and he looked pretty sad. I bet he loves you."

I wasn't just making that up. Theresa's father would know

what she was really like. He'd know her even better than I did.

"He writes every day," she said. "I never read his letters."

"Read them," I said. "You'll be glad you did."

After a pause, she said, "I didn't mind when you called me Trees, like you did before. It sounded friendly."

"I felt friendly," I said. "But don't call me Bossy Boots anymore, okay?"

"Okay," she grinned, "I'll just call my kitten Boots — after you."

Later she let me ride her new two-wheeler. She's really nice when you get to know her.

About the Author...

BRENDA BELLINGHAM is an author and former school teacher who lives in Sherwood Park, Alberta. Her numerous children's books include *Lilly's Good Deed* as well as *Lilly to the Rescue* and *Storm Child*, which was selected for the "Our Choice" Children's Book Centre Award.

About the Illustrator...

KATHY KAULBACH is a professional illustrator and designer living in Halifax. She has illustrated over 80 books, as well as *Lilly's Good Deed* and *Lilly to the Rescue.*

Another story about Lilly...

• *Lilly to the Rescue*

by Brenda Bellingham/Illustrated by
Kathy Kaulbach

Bossy-boots! That's what kids at school start
calling Lilly when she gives a lot of advice
that's not wanted. Lilly can't help telling
people what to do — but how can she keep
any of her friends if she always knows better?

Meet five other great kids in the New First Novels Series...

Meet Morgan in

• *Morgan and the Money*

by Ted Staunton/Illustrated by Bill Slavin

When money for the class trip goes
missing, Morgan wonders who to tell
about seeing Aldeen Hummel, the Godzilla
of Grade 3, at the teacher's desk with
the envelope. Morgan only wants to do
the right thing, but it's hard to know if not
telling all the truth would be the same as
telling a lie.

• *Morgan Makes Magic*

by Ted Staunton/Illustrated by Bill Slavin
When he's in a tight spot, Morgan tells stories — and most of them stretch the truth, to say the least. But when he tells kids at his new school he can do magic tricks, he really gets in trouble — most of all with the dreaded Aldeen Hummel!

Meet Jan in

• *Jan and Patch*

by Monica Hughes/Illustrated by Carlos Freire
Jan wants a puppy so badly that she would do just about anything to get one. But her mother and her gramma won't allow one in the house. So when Jan and her friend Sarah meet a puppy at the pet store, they know they have to find a creative way to make him Jan's.

• *Jan's Big Bang*

by Monica Hughes/Illustrated by Carlos Freire
Taking part in the Science Fair is a big deal for Grade 3 kids, but Jan and her best friend Sarah are ready for the challenge. Still, finding a safe project isn't easy, and the girls discover that getting ready for the fair can cause a whole lot of trouble.

Meet Carrie in

• *Carrie's Crowd*

by Lesley Choyce/Illustrated by Mark Thurman

Carrie wants to be part of the cool crowd. Becoming friends with them means getting a new image for herself but it also means ignoring her old friends. That's when Carrie starts to see that there are friends, and then there are good friends.

• *Go For It, Carrie*

by Lesley Choyce/Illustrated by Mark Thurman

More than anything else, Carrie wants to roller-blade. Her big brother and his friend just laugh at her. But Carrie knows she can do it if she just keeps trying. As her friend Gregory tells her, "You can do it, Carrie. Go for it!"

Meet Robyn in

• *Robyn's Want Ad*

by Hazel Hutchins/Illustrated by Yvonne Cathcart

Robyn is fed up with being an only child. She decides that having a part-time brother would be ideal. But the only person who answers her classified ad is her neighbour Ari and he wants Robyn to teach him piano. All she wanted was a brother, plain and simple, and now she's mixed up in Ari's plot to avoid his real piano lessons.

• *Shoot for the Moon, Robyn*

by Hazel Hutchins/Illustrated by Yvonne Cathcart

When the teacher asks her to sing for the class, Robyn knows it's her chance to be the world's best singer. Should she perform like Celine Dion, or do *My Bonnie Lies Over the Ocean*, or the matchmaker song? It's hard to decide, even for the world's best singer — and the three boys who throw spitballs don't make it any easier.

Meet Duff in

• *Duff the Giant Killer*

by Budge Wilson/Illustrated by Kim LaFave

Getting over the chicken pox can be boring, but Duff and Simon find a great way to enjoy themselves — acting out one of their favourite stories, *Jack the Giant Killer*, in the park. In fact, they do it so well the police get into the act.